Fabulous Pie

Written by Gareth Edwards ALISON GREEN BOOKS Illustrated by Guy Parker-Rees

Deep in the forest
Where the trees meet the sky,
A **very** bad bear
Baked a **very** big pie.

He made a crust of pastry
That was flaky, warm and wide,
And he had a wicked plan
To get a filling inside.

So the bear stood in a clearing
And he said with a sigh:

"Fabulous pie! Fabulous pie!
Who'll help to make the filling
For my fabulous pie?"

"Me!"
said a mouse.

"I will scamper!

I will scramble!"

And he fetched the ripest berries
From the blackberry bramble.

The bear put in the berries
And he stirred them with his paw . . .
But still he thought the pie
Needed something more.

So he clambered on a tree stump
And he asked the branches high:

"Fabulous pie! Fabulous pie!
Who'll help to make the filling
For my fabulous pie?"

"Me!" said a squirrel.
"Watch me tiptoe
on a twig!"

And she fetched
a bunch of hazelnuts,
Delicious, brown
and big.

Then the bear poured in the hazelnuts
And gave a cautious smell . . .

But he said he thought the mixture
Wasn't working very well.

So he called out down a burrow,
With a tear in his eye:

"Fabulous pie! Fabulous pie!
Who'll help to make the filling
For my fabulous pie?"

"Me!" said a badger.
"I can search the hollow trees."

And he brought a comb of honey
With a few squashed bees.

Then the bear put in the honey
And he tried a little bite . . .

But still he thought the mixture
Didn't taste exactly right.

So he called across the river
(And he sounded rather sly):

"Fabulous pie! Fabulous pie!

Who'll help to make the filling
For my fabulous pie?"

"Us," said an otter who was
Playing with her daughter . . .

And they pulled a fine, fresh salmon
From the hilly river water.

So the bear picked up the salmon
And he mixed it slowly in . . .

But still he thought the recipe
Was looking rather thin.

Then the bear put on his napkin
And he gave it one more try:

"Fabulous pie! Fabulous pie!

"Who'll help to make the filling
For my fabulous pie?"

The animals grew grumpy:

"You are being very rude!
Berries, honey, nuts and salmon!
Those are all our favourite food!"

But the bear turned to the animals
And gave a funny stare,
And he said, "I know a filling
That is **better for a bear!**"

And he shoved them in the pie crust!
Then they all began to cry:

"Terrible pie!

Terrible pie!

You **can't** make us the filling
For your terrible pie!"

Then the animals all wriggled...

And their furry paws they thrust
Through the warm and flaky pastry,

Till their legs stuck out the crust.

And off along the river bank . . .

They made a desperate dash!

Then the bear tripped
on his rolling pin

And fell **in with a** . . .

splash!

Then deep in the forest
Where the trees meet the sky,
The squirrel, mouse and badger
And the otters shared the pie.

And they all called out
As they waved goodbye
To the very bad bear
As he floated by:

"Fabulous Pie! Fabulous Pie!
How **kind** of you to bake us such a
Fabulous Pie!"

For Imogen,
who can bake a properly fabulous pie – G.E.

For Sarah,
with love from Guy x – G.P.R.

First published in the UK in 2015 by
Alison Green Books
An imprint of Scholastic Children's Books
Euston House, 24 Eversholt Street
London NW1 1DB
A division of Scholastic Ltd
www.scholastic.co.uk
London – New York – Toronto – Sydney – Auckland
Mexico City – New Delhi – Hong Kong

HB ISBN: 978 1 407131 40 5
PB ISBN: 978 1 407131 46 7

Papers used by Scholastic Children's Books are made from
wood grown in sustainable forests.